AcKaMAraCKuS

julius lester's

Sumptuously Silly Fan

AcKaMA

astically Funny Fables

raCKuS

illustrated by

emilie chollat

scholastic press new york

ISBN 0-590-48913-5
(HARDCOVER: ALK. PAPER)

Library of Congress Cataloging-in-Publication Data

Lester, Julius

Ackamarackus: Julius Lester's Sumptuously Silly

Fantastically Funny Fables/written by Julius Lester;

illustrated by Emilie Chollat.—1st ed.   p. cm.

Summary: A collection of six original fables

with morals both silly and serious.

[1. Fables. 2. Animals—Fiction.] I. Chollat. Emilie, ill.

II. Title. PZ8.2.L45 Ac 2001   [E]—dc21 00-037185

10 9 8 7 6 5 4 3 2 1   01 02 03 04 05

Printed in Singapore   46

First edition, March 2001

The display type was set in Matrix Regular,

Matrix Wide, Matrix Narrow, and Matrix Script Bold.

The text type was set in 13-point Matrix.

The illustrations were done in acrylics and collage.

Book design by Marijka Kostiw

to milan, **with** whom i *can* **be** *myself*

TABLE OF contents

HOW BERNARD THE BEE LOST HIS buzz

when Bernard the Bee woke up that morning, he yawned a couple of times and then checked his buzz. That's what bees do first thing every day. What would a bee be without a buzz? My goodness! A bee without a buzz would be a been. A bee without a buzz would be a used-to-be bee who was now a been. So Bernard buzzed his buzz a couple of times and was happy to see that *his buzz was as buzzy as it always was.*

Then he counted his black and yellow stripes. Well, that's not really true. Everybody knows bees can't count. However, if he could have counted, that's what he would have done, but because he couldn't count, he did the best he could. He looked at a yellow stripe and said, "Eighty-seven!" Next he looked at a black stripe. "One thousand sixty-four trillion." He pointed to a third stripe and announced proudly, "Nine!" Satisfied that his buzz was buzzing and all one thousand sixty-four trillion stripes were in place, **Bernard opened his wings** and went looking for breakfast.

Well, this particular morning he hadn't been flying long when he saw a field of daisies as bright as Sun after he washes his face every morning. Bernard the Bee buzzed a buzzy buzz and dived toward the daisies. But just as he was about to land, something blue flashed in the corner of his eye. He put on the brakes and it was a good thing he was wearing his seatbelt or he would have landed in the middle of next July. What do you think caused him to stop like that and forget about his breakfast? Couldn't have been anything except a girl.

Belinda Bluebird was bobbing in a birdbath wearing a burgundy bikini and just like that, *Bernard the Bee was in love.* You probably didn't know that bees fall in love, did you? Well, there is nothing on this planet that doesn't fall in love. Even rocks fall in love. I don't know how to tell you when two rocks are in love because their expressions don't change, but I do know how to tell when a bee is in love. It blushes orange and starts reciting love poems about "the birds and the people."

3

Anyway, Bernard put on the brakes, made a hard right, left, right, did a somersault, and landed on the rim of the birdbath. He was blushing so much Belinda wanted to know what kind of makeup he had on because she wouldn't mind having some lipstick that color.

"Will you marry me?" Bernard said immediately. Bees do not live long so they don't have time to take a girl out on a date or buy her chocolates and jewelry. If you are a bee you have to get with it at once.

Belinda cocked her head to one side and looked at him. He was the weirdest looking bird she had ever seen. Then again, those yellow-and-black stripes he was wearing might be the latest fashion.

"Can you swim?" Belinda wanted to know.

"Well, of course!" Bernard exclaimed, totally clueless.

"Then come on in the water. Any bird I marry has to be able to swim to keep up with me."

"Wa-wa-wa-water?" Bernard stammered. The water looked quite cold and quite wet. Then he looked at Belinda and his buzzer went bzzzzzzzzzzz and without another thought, **SPLASH!** Bernard jumped in. He coughed and flapped his wings and flopped around for a minute or two, but pretty soon he was swimming laps and doing the backstroke.

After a while Bernard was ready to buzz home and tell his parents he was in love and was going to marry Belinda Bluebird. They might find it a little odd that he, a bee, wanted to marry a bluebird, but that was love. When it comes your time, your parents might think the person you bring home is a little strange, too.

Bernard kissed Belinda good-bye, but when he opened his

wings to fly away, nothing happened.

"What's the matter?" Belinda asked, concerned.

"I don't know," Bernard answered. *"I can't seem to fly."*

He opened his wings again, expecting to feel himself float up into the air. Nothing. Then he realized it was silent. Very, very silent. When he lifted his wings he was supposed to hear his buzz. Frantically, he did his buzz test check. *Nothing. Zilch! Nada!*

Bernard turned around to look at his buzz. It was sopping, soaking wet. Bernard tried again and again to get his buzz to buzz, but poor Bernard. *His buzz had drowned.*

Without his buzz Bernard was no longer a bee. He was a been. But Belinda had fallen in love with a bird with a buzz, not a been, and when she realized that Bernard was buzzless, she flew away, leaving him all alone on the edge of the birdbath.

Poor Bernard! **What was he going to do?**

Well, the very next day his buzz was dry and he could fly again, but his buzz wouldn't buzz. And a bee without a buzz did not feel like a bee.

Bernard was very, very sad because none of the other bees recognized him. Even though he looked like a bee, he didn't *sound* like a bee. All that day Bernard flew around among all the bees, but no one would talk to him.

Bernard was about ready to cry when he heard something. "What's that?" he asked aloud.

It was the most beautiful sound he had ever heard. Bernard followed it deep inside a peony. There, sitting in the center, was a bee playing an instrument with a long neck and a body shaped like a triangle.

"Wh-who are you?" Bernard asked.

"I'm Brenda," the bee playing the instrument responded.

"And what's that you're playing?"

"It's a balalaika."

"I really love how beautiful it sounds . . . *but you're a bee!"* Bernard proclaimed. "Bees don't play balalaikas. Bees buzz."

Brenda laughed. "Any bee can buzz. But buzzing is boring. Just the same note over and over, day in and day out, month in and month out."

For the first time that day, **Bernard smiled.** "I never thought of it that way. C-can I tell you a secret?"

"Sure."

"I lost my buzz."

"You what?" Brenda exclaimed. **"Oh, my dream has come true!** I've been wishing I could find a bee without a buzz. The last thing I ever wanted was to be married to a bee who wouldn't do anything all day but buzz in that same boring note."

So Bernard and Brenda got married. He learned to play the bongos and soon, Brenda and Bernard Bee and their Balalaika Bongo Combo were playing to sold-out hives throughout the bee kingdom.

Which proves two things:

1. Always **BE ALL** *that* **YOU CAN BEE.**

2. Why buzz when **YOU CAN BALALAIKA?**

THE FLIES LEARN to fly

every year, along about the time the leaves inside the trees start to uncurl,
flies go to school. That's right! Now, I know you're probably thinking: What do
flies need to go to school for? Well, because people are always coming up with

new things like sugar-free drinks (which flies don't like), tofu ice cream (flies think it's awesome), and trout jerky (don't knock it if you haven't tried it, the flies report).

So *the flies take classes* like "Where to Find Holes in Houses," "Takeoffs and Landings," and read the latest magazines and books, such as *Martha FlyStewart's Fly Living, The Gourmet Fly's Guide to Leftovers,* and *Bug Zappers: Killers of Children.*

While in school, the flies get checkups from the school fly nurses and doctors. Having to flap their tiny wings very, very, very fast to get anywhere is exhausting. They have to watch their diets, exercise regularly, and get lots of sleep so they can stay in shape.

But one year Felicia Fly taught them something that changed being a fly forever.

"My fellow flies! Our days of wearing ourselves out by flapping our little wings are over! It is time we did what people do. You don't see them flapping their arms to get anywhere, do you?"

"Noooooo, Miss Felicia," the flies said all at once.

"When people want to go far away, how do they do it? They get inside a big fly and let it do all the flying."

The flies looked at Felicia as if they didn't have the slightest idea what she was talking about, which they didn't.

"Why, just last week I flew from Los Angeles to New York, with a changeover in Chicago, of course, in one day!" Felicia continued.

The flies could not believe their ears! None of them had ever been outside their hometowns.

"Now, think about it, fellow flies. You're hanging from the ceiling in someone's house, watching television, right?"

The flies all chuckled and nodded to each other. Hanging upside down on the ceiling and watching television was one of their favorite things.

"And suddenly you hear a voice on the television say, 'Fly American.' 'Fly United.' 'Fly Southwest.'"

The flies nodded. They had heard that. *Then, they understood* what Felicia was talking about.

"People call them 'airplanes,' but *they're nothing but giant flies!*" Felicia announced triumphantly.

Felicia didn't get a chance to say another word because the flies headed for airports, got on airplanes, and went to all the places they'd ever heard about on television and a lot they hadn't. *They had a grand time* visiting relatives they'd never seen, eating foods they never knew existed, and learning to whine in people's ears in foreign languages. But all that flying on airplanes did not make the flies lazy because they knew: A fat, lazy fly will end up as a spot on the wall.

Which proves two things:

1. *FLIES CAN DO ANYTHING they want once they put their minds to it.*

2. *THE FLY sitting on your schoolbook MIGHT BE READING it.*

HOW **THE** LION became king OF *THE* JUNGLE

lionel the Lion was the laziest lion in creation. That is saying a lot because men lions are the laziest creatures in the world. They sleep twenty hours a day!

I don't know why they're so lazy. Maybe having to carry around that big mane of hair tires them out and puts their brains to sleep. On the other hand, a lion's roar can be heard for five miles. Maybe walking around with a roar that big in their stomachs makes them drowsy. But probably, they just like to sleep.

Even during the four hours when men lions are awake, they don't do much. They spend an hour *yawning,* an hour practicing their roars, and then it's time to eat, which leaves an hour to yawn before they go back to sleep. All that yawning and roaring and eating would tire anybody out, wouldn't it?

You say you want to know just how lazy Lionel was? Lionel was too lazy to yawn. **How lazy was Lionel?** Lionel was too lazy to snore. If you want to know the truth, and I know you do, *Lionel was even too lazy to breathe.* If his lungs and heart hadn't been working on their own, Lionel would have died a long time ago.

Now, while the men lions are doing all that sleeping, *what do you think the women lions are doing?* They are out shopping, trying to chase down an antelope, zebra, or water buffalo for supper. When the women lions finally catch up to supper, wrestle it to the ground, kill it,

13

and drag it back home, guess who eats first? That's right! *Big Lazy!*

Well, one day Liora, Loretta, and Letty Lion, who were all married to Lionel, got tired of the situation. They wanted to do something about it, but what? They thought and thought and then thought some more.

Finally, Liora Lion said, "Why don't we ask some of our friends what they think we should do about Lionel?"

"Great idea!" Loretta Lion agreed.

"Whom shall we talk to first?" Letty asked.

"Let's go see our good friend Henrietta Hippopotamus," Liora suggested. Letty and Loretta thought that was a fine idea, so off they went to the river to see Henrietta Hippopotamus.

When they found Henrietta, she was just finishing her morning mudbath.

"Henrietta, we're tired of Lionel being so lazy, *but we don't know what to do* about it."

Henrietta Hippopotamus thought for a moment. **"I could sit on him,"** she finally said. "That would scare him so much he'd jump up and run for a hundred miles."

Liora, Lorretta, and Letty had never seen Lionel walk ten *feet*. They could not imagine him running. But it was worth a try.

"All right," they told Henrietta, and off they went to where Lionel was sleeping.

When Henrietta saw Lionel, sleeping as serenely as moonlight shining on a lake, she shook her head. *"I'm sorry, ladies.* I — I like the idea, but I can't do it. I have never seen anyone enjoy himself as much as Lionel enjoys sleeping. I wish I could enjoy mudbathing as much." And Henrietta went home.

"What're we going to do now?" Letty Lion wanted to know.

"Let's go see Elizabeth Elephant. **She's very smart!** She'll know what to do," Loretta said.

When they told Elizabeth what they wanted, she said, "Well, I could pick him up with my trunk and twirl him around a few times. *That should put some get-up-and-go in him.*"

Liora, Loretta, and Letty thought that was a wonderful idea. So they took

Elizabeth Elephant to the place where Lionel was sleeping.

When Elizabeth saw Lionel lying in the grass as still as a raindrop on a leaf, she shook her head. "I'm sorry, ladies, but I can't do it. **Look at him!** He's not just sleeping. He is putting his heart and his soul into it! I wish there was something I cared about so much." And Elizabeth left.

Liora, Loretta, and Letty took a new look at Lionel, and they realized that Henrietta Hippopotamus and Elizabeth Elephant were right! Lionel was not just lazy. *He was a genius* at it! No lion in liohistory had ever been as brilliantly lazy as Lionel.

"He *is* beautiful, isn't he?" Liora said, with awe in her voice.

Loretta and Letty agreed. "Instead of trying to change him, I think the whole world should know about *Lionel's greatness!*" Letty exclaimed.

"What a wonderful idea!" Loretta agreed. "What should we do?"

"I know!" Liora exclaimed. "First we have to make a sign."

No, I do not know where they got the cardboard and the paints and the hammer and nails for the sign. Probably the same place you do — the basement! And yes, lions can read and write as well as anybody. *Everybody knows that!*

When the sign was ready, they stuck it in the ground next to Lionel. Then Liora said, "Okay. Now, let's hide in the tall grasses!"

Before long, a van filled with tourists came along, and when the driver saw the sign, he stopped. *"Look!"* he announced to the tourists.

The tourists saw the sign and got very excited, and they rushed out of the van with their cameras.

"Look at him!" exclaimed Ozzie from Oxnard.

"What a magnificent mane of hair!" exulted Patricia from Petaluma.

Each tourist put a dollar on the ground next to Lionel and took many pictures of him.

"This is the real thing!" expounded Gustav from Göteborg. "The King of the Jungle!"

When the tourists got back in the van and drove away, Liora, Loretta, and Letty came out of the high grasses, picked up the money, and counted it. While it is true that lions can read and write, they cannot count past one. So Liora, Loretta, and Letty did not know how much money they had, but they knew it was a lot of ones and that they were going to be making many more of them.

Which proves two things:

1. APPRECIATE SOMEBODY for who he is instead of getting upset about who he isn't.

2. You can BE A GENIUS at anything.

ANNA THE angry ANT

anna the Ant was ambling along one day looking for a shoe store. Her feet hurt — all six of them. Every other creature had been born with shoes. Well, maybe not shoes exactly, but they had something to protect their feet — claws or pads or skin — *something!* Because ants, caterpillars, and centipedes have more legs than anybody, they have more feet. But do they have shoes? No! Do their feet hurt? ***You'd better believe it!*** Crawling over rocks and dirt and leaves and trees all day with no shoes or skin on would make anybody's feet hurt. Just thinking about it made Anna the Ant turn into Anna the Angry Ant, and the last thing you ever want to do is mess with an angry ant (of which there are quite a few).

Suddenly there was a noise. It sounded like Thunder had come down from Sky to see what Rain had been doing.

"Who's there?" Anna shouted. Although ants are small, they can be very, very loud. Like you are sometimes.

"Who's making all that racket?" came back a voice as tiny as a snowflake.

"You'd better show yourself," Anna yelled, "or *I'll eat you up!*"

Anna waited tensely until, suddenly, there appeared the biggest, largest, hugest, giantest, humongousest snake Anna had ever seen. It was ***Anadama the Anaconda.***

Now, between you and me, I don't ever want to see an anaconda. It is the biggest snake on the sunshine side of tomorrow. That snake is so long its tail is in Monday and its eyes are looking into next Tuesday.

When Anadama the Anaconda saw what had been yelling at her, she said, "Miss Ant, *you're hardly bigger than a gnat's eyelash.* Do you really think you can eat me up? I am twenty-five feet long and weigh five hundred pounds. Just what do you think you can do to me?"

Anadama the Anaconda should not have said that. Not on a day when Anna's six feet hurt and she was hot and tired from looking for a shoe store

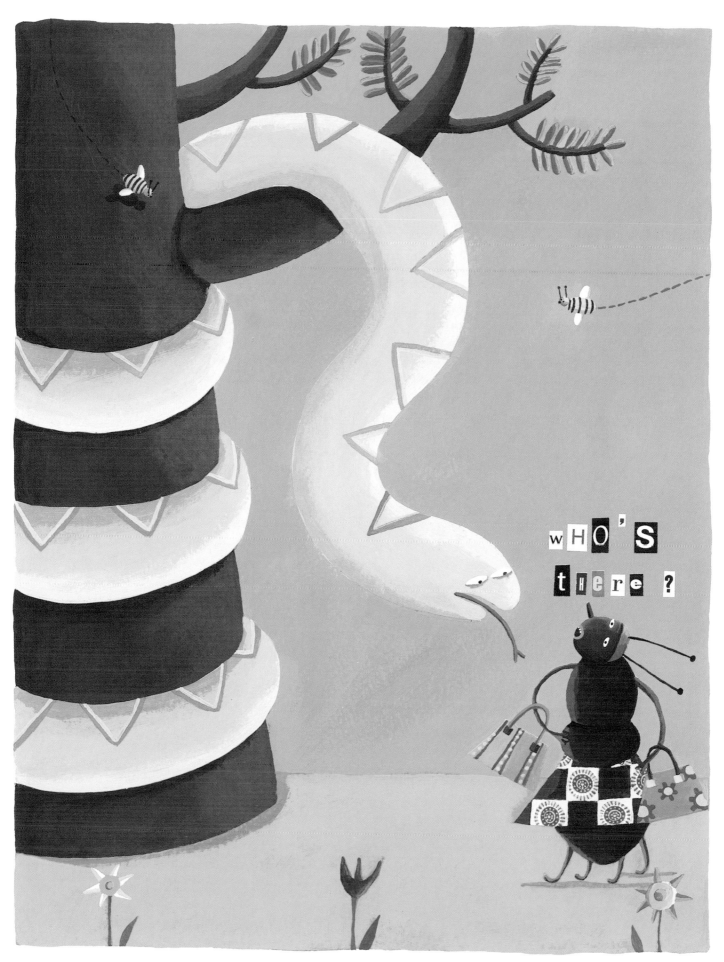

21

and now wanted nothing more than to find a picnic so she could have some cold iced tea. No, this was not the day for an overweight snake to be messing with her!

Anna opened her mouth *wider than a wish,* and before Anadama knew what was happening, she was history. That's right! Anna the Angry Ant slurped and swallowed Anadama the Anaconda like she was *a strand of spaghetti.*

However, that turned out to be a mistake. A big mistake! Anna's abdomen ached achingly for the rest of her life and, seeing as how a female ant can live to be fourteen years old, that's a lot of aching.

Which proves two things:

1. DON'T EAT WHEN YOU'RE ANGRY.
   You might swallow more than you want to.

2. If you ever see an ant in your shoes,
   it's only TRYing THEM ON FOR SIZE.

ELLEN *THE* EAGLE finds **her** place IN THE WORLD

when Ellen the Eagle was born, her first word was " H E E E E E E L P ! "

That was because the first thing she saw was the ground. But she was not on it.

Ellen was teetering on the lip of a ledge high, high, high on a mountaintop.

"Get me down from here!" she demanded. "And I mean *NOW!*"

"You're an eagle, dear," said her mother, Edie, putting a wing around the baby bird to protect her. "You don't want to live down there with things like sparrows and pigeons."

"This eagle wants a condo on the beach in Hawaii," Ellen shot back.

"You'll get used to it," Eddie, her father, put in. *"One day you'll be soaring in the clouds."*

"There's no ground up there. In fact, I don't see anything up there. How am I supposed to walk around on blue nothing?"

"You won't walk. You'll fly — with these." And Edie opened her great wings.

"Yikes!" Ellen exclaimed. "You mean I've got to carry those around all the time?"

"Aren't they magnificent?"

"You're nuts!"

Being born an eagle didn't mean that that was what Ellen wanted to be.

Ellen learned to fly, but she didn't like it. For one thing, it was cold way up there with the clouds. Flying was also boring. There was nothing to do except go around and around and around in circles. Not only that, *flying did not make sense.*

"What's holding me up?" she asked herself. "Air, right? But *what is air?* What if I'm soaring around up here bored out of my skull one day and the air decides it doesn't like me? Or maybe the air will think it's more impor- tant to hold up some other bird, a junco, for crying out loud. Or maybe the air will get tired of having to be everywhere at the same time and take a vacation. After all, the air has been here since the world was born. It has been going in and out of the lungs and cells of people and animals and plants and water. You have to admit that being air is kind of **a yuck job. And boring!"**

Suddenly, Ellen wondered if the air had been listening. What if the air disappeared right that second? Terrified that was what was going to happen, Ellen quickly dropped from the sky and onto the branch of an old dead tree. *"That's it!"* Ellen declared. "I am not going up in the air ever again. The air doesn't like me and I don't like it!"

Ellen did not know that she looked very regal and noble sitting there in the tree. But not having a mirror, Ellen didn't know she had any looks at all.

Just then a park ranger named Ellen came hiking by. **"Wow! Isn't that eagle magnificent?"** she exclaimed.

Ellen wondered, *Is she talking about me? Me? Magnificent?*

Ellen the Ranger admired Ellen the Eagle's beauty for a moment more and then she resumed hiking up the trail.

"Stop!" Ellen the Eagle yelled, but it came out as **"Awk!** You can't leave me here. I'm no good as an eagle. I'm a rotten eagle. I'll die out here in the woods. Don't you know the air is going to go away and the clouds are going to fall and hit everybody on the head?!" Ellen was jumping up and down and flapping her wings trying to get Ellen's attention, when suddenly she lost her balance and, with a *loud screech,* fell out of the tree, hit her head on a rock, and knocked herself out.

Sometime later Ellen woke up. **Where am I?** she wondered, feeling warm and cozy, lying in bed beneath a blanket. Her eyes popped open and she saw Ellen looking down at her. Ellen smiled eaglerly. Of course, when an eagle smiles it looks like it is going to rip your heart out of your chest.

Ellen the Ranger jumped back. Ellen the Eagle knew she had done something wrong, so she turned her head away. After a moment, Ellen the Ranger came closer and, sitting down on the edge of the bed, she held out her hand and began gently stroking Ellen's feathers. Ellen sighed deeply and was soon asleep.

The next morning Ellen took Ellen outside.

"You're all better now," she said. "It's time for you to return to nature."

"Are you nuts?" Ellen said. "Nature is no place for an animal. Everything looks at everything else and all they see is dinner." And *she promptly fainted.*

Ellen the Ranger was upset. "Maybe she's weaker than I realized from that bump on her head."

She took Ellen back inside and radioed her boss and asked what to do with the eagle she had found.

"You won't believe this!" her boss exclaimed. "I just got a call from the President. He says that the eagle they have been using to pose for pictures on postage stamps and posters and in television commercials is unhappy and wants to go soar in the beautiful, spacious skies."

"Fantastic!" Ellen responded. "I have a feeling this eagle wants nothing to do with any spacious skies or purple mountains' majesty."

When Ellen heard that, she opened her eyes but kept her smile to herself.

The President sent his own plane to get Ellen and Ellen and fly them to Washington, D.C. To this day, they live in a penthouse apartment near the White House. Whenever anybody in the government needs a picture of an eagle for a stamp or anything official, a photographer comes to the apartment.

Ellen puts on her noblest look and the photographer takes her picture.

Now everyone knows eagles have very sharp eyesight. What people don't know is that clouds have sharp eyesight, too. Which is how Ellen's parents learned *she had a job.* One day they were soaring up in the sky where all the blue color is made. A cloud drifted over and told them that she had seen their daughter's picture on the side of a mail truck.

"Ellen's picture on the side of a truck?" Edie and Eddie said together.

They flew around until they spotted a mail truck.

"Look at her, Eddie!" Edie said proudly.

"I'd recognize that beak anywhere," Eddie agreed.

And they were very proud that their daughter had followed her mind.

Which proves two things:

1. *If you were born a chicken but think you're an eagle, DON'T BE A TURKEY!*

2. **Make sure you're on the ground the day the air decides to TAKE A VACATION.**

THE incredible adventure of ADALBERT THE alligator

it was hot in the swamp that summer. It was so hot the frogs had to watch a National Geographic special to remember how to hop. It was so hot mosquitoes drank lemonade. It was so hot that one day, Adalbert the Alligator discovered he was swimming in sweat instead of water, and that was when he decided to move to Vermont.

However, *Adalbert had a problem.* He didn't know where Vermont was. Well, if there is any somebody in nature who knows everything, it is the birds who are always flying hither to get to yon.

Adalbert envied birds because they were cute and people fed them all the time. He remembered a time when birds worked for a living and dug for worms. This new generation of birds didn't do anything but fly from bird feeder to bird feeder. He, on the other hand, had to work for a living. No one was putting alligator feeders in their backyards.

Adalbert could've gone to a zoo or alligator farm and eaten all the fish he wanted for the rest of his life. But that would not have made up for people staring at him and talking about how ugly he was.

Alligators know they are ugly. You cannot be that ugly and not know it. Alligators have tried wigs and makeup and if you want to see something that is truly ugly, it is an alligator in a blonde wig. Being so ugly meant they didn't have any friends. *Well, that's not exactly true.* They didn't have any friends because they ate them. But they couldn't stop doing that any more than they could stop being ugly. Which was why Adalbert wasn't sure if the birds would help him. He had eaten quite a few of them.

Well, he wouldn't know if they would help until he asked. Because he could not get close enough to a bird to say anything, he talked to the birds' closest friend, a tree.

"Listen. *I need a favor from the birds,*" he said to the tree.

"What kind of favor?" the tree wanted to know.

"I want to go to Vermont but I don't know where it is."

"What will you do for the birds if they help you?"

"Anything they want."

"I'll pass the word."

The birds were immediately suspicious. What would an alligator do in Vermont? Especially when it started snowing! Suddenly, the birds thought: *An alligator in Vermont in February under four feet of snow?* The thought put a smile on their beaks.

The birds called a big meeting. Custer Cuckoo flew in from Curaçao. Patsy Parrot was there from Pittsburgh. (That wasn't good because her ex-husband, Peter Parrot from Paramus, was there with his new wife, Corrie Cockatiel from Colchester.) And Velma Virago came from — where else? — **Vermont.**

The birds talked for a long time before they reached a decision. Crandall Crow from Colorado, the Bird President, went to Adalbert. "Here's the deal. We will help you get to Vermont if you agree not to eat birds anymore."

Adalbert blinked his big eyes. *"You're joking!"* Birds were one of the tastiest things in creation! "I don't know, Crandall. That's asking a lot."

"Take it or leave it."

Adalbert was silent for a moment. "Have you been to Vermont, Crandall?"

"Sure have."

"Is it true that it's not hot up there?"

"Not like down here."

That settled it. "Crandall, it's a deal."

The next morning, Adalbert started out for Vermont. The first day, Roscoe Robin was his guide. Because birds flew everywhere and saw everything, they

34

knew a lot but seldom got a chance to tell anyone all they knew, so that first day *Roscoe gave Adalbert a lecture* on the Florida Everglades and their relationship to the ecosystem of the Caribbean. Adalbert had no idea what Roscoe was talking about and wondered if it would be all right to eat the birds that talked too much.

Finally, many days, many birds, and many lectures later, Nell the Nuthatch said, **"This is Vermont, Adalbert.** Take care of yourself."

"Where're you going, Nell?" Adalbert asked nervously.

"I've got to get the husband and kids ready for winter."

"Winter? What's that?"

Nell laughed a nuthatchey laugh. "You'll find out." And she flew away.

Adalbert was all alone. The Vermont birds had been expecting him and they let the other birds know. "The dumb alligator from Florida has arrived," a crow called.

Adalbert's feelings were hurt. Just because he was ugly didn't mean he was dumb. It wasn't his fault that it didn't take many brains to be an alligator. **He was still a very fine alligator.**

Adalbert went deep into the forest until he came to a lake and slipped into the water. It was colder than the water in Florida, but because he was cold-blooded, his body temperature adjusted quickly and he settled himself comfortably on the rocky bottom. Once a week or so, he floated to the top and looked around to be sure Vermont was still there. It always was.

But one afternoon when he came up, something was different. **Oh, my goodness!** The leaves weren't green anymore!

Adalbert rushed out of the water and looked this way and that. The sun shining through the red, orange, and yellow leaves made the air shimmer and shine with color. Adalbert found a beautiful patch of yellow air and lay down. He wanted to go back and tell the other alligators about this place called Vermont where you could be a color. *In Vermont, even an alligator was beautiful.*

So Adalbert was yellow for a few days, then red, then orange for a few more, and yellow again, and thus it went until one morning, he noticed the yellow and red and orange leaves were falling to the ground and the air was not colored anymore.

"What's the matter?" Adalbert asked a tree. *"You stopped liking your leaves?"*

"No," the tree responded. "It's almost time for us to go to sleep for the winter."

"Winter? What's that?"

The tree chuckled. "Oh, you'll know when it comes."

Adalbert was sad that the trees were throwing away all their leaves. Why would they do that? If he was covered with orange leaves and looked so beautiful, he wouldn't change for anything. But the trees became bare, and the air grew cold as if it was angry about not being dressed in pretty colors any longer.

One morning soon after the trees had dropped all their leaves, Adalbert felt something cold and wet on his snout. *Pieces of fluff were falling,* but unlike rain, they were quiet. They were so quiet. Adalbert was scared. What was the white fluff going to do?

Soon he knew. It was going to cover everything, including him, if he didn't

WHat's the MATTeR?

find somewhere to hide. Adalbert scurried through the forest trying to get away from the white fluff, but alligators are big, and *where in a forest could an alligator hide?*

Adalbert climbed a mountain, but the snow and ice and cold made him tired and weak. He was finding it hard to breathe. Adalbert didn't love Vermont anymore and wished he were back in Florida swimming in sweat. Just as his eyes started to close for the last time, he heard a voice.

"You are the oddest creature I've ever seen."

Adalbert opened his eyes. A big, furry animal was standing in front of him.

37

"What are you?" Adalbert whispered. "You don't look so normal yourself."

"I'm Bertice Bear."

Adalbert's eyes opened wider. "Bertice. My name's Adalbert. Our names are almost the same."

"Bertice. Adalbert. Adalbert. Bertice." The bear nodded. "So, I know your name but I don't know what you are."

"I'm an alligator, of course."

"And what's an alligator?"

Adalbert was stumped. Where he lived, everybody knew what he was. "Well, I'm like a snake, I guess, but a lot bigger."

Bertice looked at Adalbert more closely. "Snakes are ugly. You're not."

"I beg your pardon?"

"You have a long snout and long pretty teeth and look at those gorgeous eyes! I like your long tail, too. And what pretty feet! I love **pretty feet!"**

To tell the truth, Adalbert wondered if Bertice was a little whacked. On the other hand, he was not about to reject a compliment, the only one he had ever heard in his life.

"Where do you live?" Bertice asked.

"Well, that's just it. I'm homeless."

"I've got plenty of room in my cave. You can stay all winter if you want."

"You mean it?" Adalbert couldn't believe his ears.

"Let's go."

Adalbert followed Bertice around the side of the mountain until there, beneath a ledge near the top, was the opening of the cave.

"Make yourself at home," Bertice said, once they were inside.

39